DRAWING

Patience Foster

Edited by Lynn Myring

Designed by Iain Ashman

Illustrated by Patience Foster, Martin Newton, Rob McCaig, Stuart Knowles, Graham Smith, Joan Selwood/Garden Studio, Gordon Wylie, Robert Ashby.

Contents

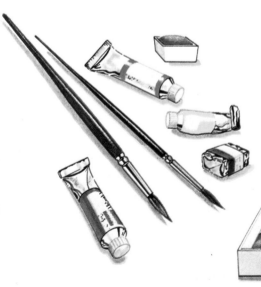

About this book

People are often disappointed with their first sketches or drawings and find the choice of materials on sale rather bewildering. This book is a guide to different materials, showing how they can be used and the effects that they create. It also explains the basic rules and techniques of drawing which will help you through the early stages.

   Remember that it takes time and practice to learn any new skill and that a single picture can sometimes take a long time to complete. Most people enjoy the process of drawing for its own sake as well as for the picture it produces.

Patience Foster drew the picture on this page, the flowers on page 12, the seascape on page 15, the still life on page 24 and scenes on pages 22 and 23.

First published in 1981 by Usborne Publishing Ltd, 20 Garrick Street, London WC2E 9BJ. Copyright © 1981 Usborne Publishing Ltd.

Printed by Casterman, S.A., Tournai, Belgium.

The name Usborne and the device are Trade Marks of Usborne Publishing Ltd.

Choosing drawing materials

The next three pages describe the most commonly available drawing materials and illustrate the sort of marks they make. Most drawing materials are made from a mixture of "pigment" and "medium". The pigment is the colour which makes the mark on the paper and is very soft and powdery. The medium is usually a sort of gum which binds the pigment together.

Different drawing materials are made from different proportions of pigment and medium. Some are soft and dusty and contain more pigment than medium. Harder materials have a higher proportion of medium.

4B 2B B
HB H 2H

Pencils

Pencils are made from a mixture of graphite (pigment) and clay (medium) encased in a tube of wood. It is worth buying good quality, named brands of pencil. Bad pencils feel hard and gritty to use and make pale marks. All good pencils are graded by a letter and number which show how hard or soft they are. "H" pencils are hard, "B" pencils are soft and "HB" and "F" pencils are a medium grade, between the two. The higher the number with the letter, the more extreme the hardness or softness. The hardest is 10H and the softest 9B – each grade makes a different effect. It is a good idea to buy several different grades of pencil and to experiment with them.

Erasers

There are many kinds of eraser on sale. Some have a special purpose such as removing ink marks. Most work by removing the top surface of the paper, which leaves a poorer surface to draw on. The best sort of eraser for pencil and charcoal is a kneadable putty eraser as it will not damage the paper too much. Putty erasers are very soft and can be moulded into a point.

India eraser

Putty eraser

Ink eraser

Sharpeners

Some manufacturers actually recommend that their pencils are sharpened with a knife rather than a sharpener. If you use a craft knife to sharpen pencils you will be able to make a useful chisel-shaped point on the lead. A block of sand- or glass-paper strips is good for keeping a point on charcoal or conté sticks and pencils, or very soft lead pencils.

Pencil sharpener

Craft knife

Sand-paper block

Charcoal

Charcoal is made from carbonized (specially burned) wood, usually willow or vine twigs. It is a very soft and dusty material which smudges easily and is always black.

Charcoal is sold in a variety of forms. Pure charcoal comes as sticks in thin, medium and thick widths. Compressed charcoal is hard as it is a mixture of charcoal and a medium. It is sold in regular shaped sticks and is also made into pencils ranging from soft to hard.

Finished drawings should be "fixed" with a spray-on fixative to prevent the charcoal smudging (see page 9).

Conté crayons

Conté crayons are short, square-ended sticks made from a special kind of compressed chalk. They are available in black, white, several shades of grey and three earthy brown colours. You can also buy conté in pencil form.

Conté is similar to charcoal in many respects, being a soft and dusty material. It makes thick, grainy marks which are easy to smudge so finished drawings should be sprayed with fixative.

Conté crayons and charcoal are very fragile and should be kept in a box with some protective packing when not being used.

Conté pencil

Conté sticks

3

Coloured drawing materials

There are many kinds of coloured drawing materials to choose from and some are very bright and vivid. They are slighty more expensive than black and white materials but most good quality crayons and paints are sold individually as well as in sets, so you can build up a range of colours gradually. It is worth buying good quality materials as they contain the best pigment and so have better colours than cheap ranges.

Soft pencil

Thin, hard pencil

Water-soluble pencil

Coloured pencils

Coloured pencils contain a mixture of pigments, clay and medium. There are several different kinds of good quality pencil and many art stores will let you try them out before you choose which to buy. You could buy one of each kind to see which you prefer.

Some pencils have quite thick leads which make soft, grainy lines. Others (sometimes called "veri-thin") have harder, thinner leads and are designed to draw fine lines. You can also buy water-soluble pencils which draw lines that dissolve to make a blurred effect or an area of flat colour if a wash of clean water is put on top.

Fibre tipped pens

Fibre tipped pens are available in a wide range of bright colours and a variety of different shaped tips. Some have quite hard, thin tips and make fine lines, others have chisel-shaped tips that can draw thick and fine lines. Many pens have a rounded tip which makes a broad, even mark. You can also buy short, chunky pens, which are good for filling in large areas of colour.

Most pens contain a spirit-based ink which will not run if another colour is put on top. A few pens use water-soluble ink which can be used with a wash of water. Both kinds evaporate quickly so replace pen tops as soon as possible.

Pastels

Pastels are small sticks of soft, pure pigment mixed with a little binding gum. They are very soft and crumbly which makes them rather difficult to draw with until you get used to them. The best quality "Artists' " pastels come in a huge range of colours, three grades of softness and are very expensive.

It is a good idea to start with a small box of a cheaper kind of pastel as these are harder than Artists' quality pastels and so are easier to use. You can also buy a sort of pastel in pencil form but these are less versatile than the sticks.

Oil pastels

Oil pastels look similar to soft pastels but they are very different in feel and effect. Oil pastels are made from oil, pigment and a binding medium and are quite firm, not powdery and crumbly like soft pastels. They come in a range of strong, bright colours which give thick, solid cover and are best used in a bold style. Oil pastels are also much cheaper than ordinary pastels.

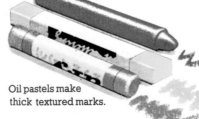

Oil pastels make thick textured marks.

Water-soluble waxy crayon

Wax crayons

Wax crayons are cheap and readily available. They are made in many bright colours and various thicknesses. It is worth buying the more expensive makes of wax crayon sold in art stores as they have a much better texture and colour than cheap kinds. There are also some waxy textured water-soluble crayons which can be used with washes of water.

Pens

The two main kinds of drawing pen are dip pens and fountain pens. Both kinds usually have changeable nibs which make lines of varying widths. Make sure you buy drawing nibs, as writing nibs are not so flexible and are not very good for drawing. Dip pens are cheaper than fountain pens, which can be filled with ink. Mapping pens are small dip pens with fine nibs.

You can also buy special technical drawing pens from art stores, such as the "Rotring" pen. Their nibs look like fine wire and draw a very even line. They are quite expensive.

Paints

Water-colour paints can be very useful for adding a wash of colour to a pencil or pen drawing. You can buy water-colours in tubes or pans, individually and in boxes. They are quite expensive but you will probably need only a few colours.

Mapping pen

Dip pen

Fountain pen

Rotring pen

Inks

You will find several kinds of drawing ink on sale in art stores. Indian ink is the best if you want a deep black, but you can also buy inks in a range of colours. Coloured inks can be lightened by mixing with distilled water.

Many inks are waterproof once they have dried and so will not run if you put a new colour on top of them. As ink is transparent the first colour will show through the second.

You can also buy non-waterproof inks, made for use in fountain pens. These inks do run if one colour is put on top of another, even after the ink has dried.

Brushes

If you use paint or water-soluble crayons you will need some paint brushes for applying the washes. Good quality hair brushes, such as sable or squirrel, are the best although rather expensive.

Large, soft brushes are very good for flat washes. You can also try drawing directly with a brush and paint or ink. Small or medium-sized brushes are best for line work and will draw broad or fine strokes

Water-colour brushes taper to a point.

Papers

Choosing paper can be difficult as there are so many different types. You can buy paper in pads of varying sizes, or as single sheets. It is a good idea to buy a few sheets of different papers and try them out. The main choice is between rough and smooth surfaced papers. Rough papers are good for materials like charcoal and conté which show up the texture of paper. Smooth paper allows more precise, detailed drawing, especially with pen and ink or pencil. Pastels should be used on paper with a rough texture (called a tooth) which will hold the grains of pastel. The different thicknesses of paper are called "weights".

Pastel papers are specially made for use with soft pastels. They are good quality and quite expensive.

"Ingres" pastel paper

Rough cartridge paper

H.P. water-colour paper

Sugar paper

Cartridge paper is a comparatively cheap paper. It is cream or white and varies from slightly rough to smooth.

Water-colour paper is made in three textures: hot pressed or H.P. which is very smooth; rough which is a textured paper and Not (not hot pressed) which is between these two.

Sugar paper is a cheap, often strongly coloured, rough paper. It is good for charcoal, conté and crayons.

Starting to draw

Easels are used more for painting than drawing.

You will have a better view of the subject and your drawing if you prop your drawing board up, rather than have it flat on the table.

A sketch pad is often the most convenient surface to draw on.

When you are drawing you need to rest your paper on a firm, smooth surface. A sketch pad with a thick cardboard back is good if you are making quick sketches or a small drawing. For larger or more detailed pictures you may find a drawing board propped up at a slope on a table more comfortable to work at.

Most drawing boards are made from wood and are rather expensive. Try using a sheet of plywood or very thick card instead. Always fix your paper to the board with masking tape or clips, as pins make holes which spoil the drawing surface. To get a very smooth surface, put some thick paper between the board and your drawing paper. Easels can be useful if you are working with dusty materials such as pastels or charcoal.

Learning to look

Learning to look carefully at the subject you are drawing is as important as learning to use different materials or rules about proportions and perspective. For this reason you should try to draw from life whenever possible and train yourself to draw what you see, not what you think you see. This picture shows some of the things to look out for when drawing from life.

The direction of the light is very important as it affects all the shadows and highlights. If you do not draw from life it is difficult to get the effect consistent on all the objects in a picture.

Shadows help to make an object look solid. If you do not include shadows and highlights in a drawing, it will look flat. You can tell that the mug is an open cylinder because of the shine and shadow inside the rim.

On the curved surface of the orange, the effects of light and shadow are gradual. Shadows on the flat table are more uniform.

Shadows form suddenly at sharp edges, making a complex pattern of light and dark.

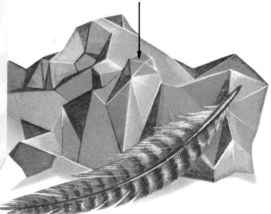

The rough texture of the orange's skin picks up shadow and light. The colour seems to change as well.

The mug has a shiny surface so it reflects the colour of the orange.

Look for the main shapes and patterns of the things you are drawing. If you get these right your picture will look realistic.

Although you know that the blue of these stripes is uniform all round, it looks different in various places because of the effects of light, shadow and coloured reflections.

Even the most familiar and simple things which you see and use every day are best drawn from life. If you try to draw from memory you will find it hard to make your picture look convincing. This is because you have probably never looked closely enough at the small details to be able to remember and reproduce them. You have to learn to do this by practising.

Measuring and proportions

Your drawings will look more life-like if you are able to draw the subject so that it has the same proportions as the real thing. It is difficult to do this just by looking. For example, if you are drawing a house, you may make it too wide for its height, or put the door in the wrong place in relation to the windows. The best way of making your observations more precise is to measure and compare the sizes and positions of the things you are drawing. You can do this very easily using a pencil as a measuring device in the way shown below.

Stand away from your subject. Hold a pencil upright straight out in front of you, keeping your arm stiff all the time.

Close one eye and line up the end of the pencil with the top of the thing you are measuring, in this case, the door of the house.

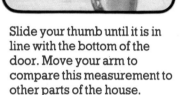

House is 3 doors high.

Slide your thumb until it is in line with the bottom of the door. Move your arm to compare this measurement to other parts of the house.

Check that the proportions of your drawing are similar to the proportions of the things you are drawing.

Notice the slope and angle of roof when compared to the upright walls.

Check the windows to see if they are all the same height and width.

These windows and the door all line up with each other horizontally and vertically.

Look at how the windows line up with each other.

Compare the height of the house with its width.

You can also use a pencil to see if things line up both horizontally and vertically. Hold it out in front of you with your arm straight as shown above, but instead of sliding your thumb to get a measurement, use the pencil as a straight line.

When you have found things which line up, sketch some light pencil lines on your drawing to help you get the positions right.

Notice how tall the bushes are when compared to the house.

Keeping a sketchbook

Practice is very important when you are learning to draw. It is a good idea to carry a small sketch pad or book around with you so that you can make quick sketches of objects and scenes which catch your eye. You can also use it for trying out new drawing materials and techniques. If you prefer to work on pieces of loose paper, stick them into a scrap book when you have finished.

It is very useful to keep a record of your sketches and experiments. You can use them when planning more detailed pictures and as references to work from later. Looking at other artists' work will also give you lots of ideas for pictures and help you find new ways of drawing. Your local library will probably have some books illustrated with the work of famous artists.

Basic techniques

Here are some guidelines which will help you to get started in drawing. There are no hard and fast rules. You will develop your own techniques and style of drawing with experiment and practice. Most of the techniques here are illustrated in pencil but they can be applied to other materials.

1 Building up a drawing

Starting a drawing can be rather daunting. The best way to begin is by drawing a simple rough sketch which shows the positions and sizes of all the things you want in the picture. Use very light strokes to make pale, faint marks and do not worry about detail yet.

2 Use lots of light marks to build up dark areas rather than heavy marks.

Next, put in some details and begin to build up areas of shade with very light, almost feathery strokes. These will be easy to cover up or erase later if you make a mistake. Always build up a drawing gradually and keep looking at your subject while you work.

3

Try to work on the drawing as a whole, if you concentrate on one part at a time it may not fit together very well by the end. When you shade or colour one part go on to all the other areas which are a similar tone, this will help to get the contrasts and balance right.

Creating light and dark tones

This picture shows some different ways of making dark and light tone. Although all nine techniques are used to show the same thing – a tree – each method creates a different impression and effect. Try out these techniques with different drawing materials. Of course most drawings are a combination of several techniques, not just one alone.

Curved line – helps to give an impression of solid roundness to the tree. This is sometimes called directional line.

Stipple – small dots placed close together.can be used to make tone. Vary the size and spacing of dots for different effects.

Reverse drawing – here the tone is uniform, smooth pencil shading and a putty eraser has been used to pick out the white highlights.

Cross-hatching – two sets of hatching, one crossing on top of the other at an angle. This makes a darker tone than just hatching.

Hatching – parallel lines quite close together. You can vary the length, spacing and weight of the line to make different tones.

Directional line – follows the growth of the tree. The lines on the trunk give an impression of bark textures too.

Solid tone – looks rather unnatural and abstract in effect.

Graduated shading – varies from light to dark and can be made by smudging a soft mark gently or by varying the pressure with which you apply the crayon or pencil.

Wash – graduated tone created with watery paint or ink, or clean water over soluble crayon lines.

Working with pencils

Ordinary pencils are probably the most versatile and easy to use drawing materials. They are very convenient for making quick sketches as well as for detailed precise drawings. Here are some hints on drawing with pencils.

Pencils work best when they are sharp, so have a sharpener or craft knife handy when drawing, or use a strip of sand-paper to keep a point on your pencils. Soft pencils are rather smudgy

and it is a good idea to keep a sheet of clean paper under your hand as you draw to help prevent smudging and to keep the paper clean. Try holding your pencil further away from the point than you do when writing. This allows you to make more flowing strokes and gives you a better view of your drawing as it will not be hidden by your hand.

Making corrections

Never expect every line and mark you make to be perfect. You will have to re-draw and possibly rub out many of your original lines to get your drawing right. This is why you should use light marks and build up a picture gradually.

When you make a mistake do not rush to erase it but draw over the wrong lines. They will show where you went wrong and help you to get it right. Mistakes can be covered by new lines or areas of tone later. Leave most of the rubbing out until the end and then erase all the marks that you feel the picture would be better without.

Fixing drawings

Pencil drawings tend to smudge easily unless they are sprayed with a layer of fixative. It is probably not worth fixing every sketch but only the drawings you want to keep, especially if they are on sheets of loose paper or drawn with soft pencil. You can buy fixative in aerosol sprays or as a liquid to use with a mouth-operated diffuser, as shown below.

Diffuser

A diffuser is made from two thin tubes hinged together in the middle. Place one end in the liquid fixative, then bend the other tube at a right angle and steadily blow through it. This sends a fine mist of fixative through the hole between the two tubes. Stand about half a metre away from the picture.

Choosing pencils

Different grades of pencil create different kinds of effect and it is worth using more than one grade when drawing with pencil. A collection of 4B, 2B, B, HB, H and 2H would be useful for most general sketching. This picture shows how some pencils could be used together.

These clouds were softly shaded with a 2B pencil. The grain of the paper helps to make a light, airy effect.

The dense dark vegetation in the foreground was shaded with soft 4B and 2B pencils.

The buildings and trees in the middle of the picture were drawn with sharp HB and B pencils which are less dark and smudgy than 2B and 4B pencils.

Using colour

Choosing colours when you are drawing is really a matter of personal taste. Some people like to use mixtures of vivid colours, others prefer softer, more harmonious colours. Colours do have certain characteristics though, and can be used to draw attention to part of a picture or to give it a mood or feeling. You do not have to copy exactly the colours of the things you are drawing, but you can try to use colours creatively. You will give a picture a quite different effect if you use bright, pure colours rather than softer, more subtle shades mixed together. These pages will help you to learn how to use colour.

Primary colours

There are three basic colours, red, blue and yellow, which can make any other colour when mixed together but which cannot themselves be made by mixing other colours. These three colours are called "primary colours".

Secondary colours

Orange, green and purple are called "secondary colours". These are made by mixing equal amounts of two primary colours together. Orange is a mixture of red and yellow, green a mixture of blue and yellow and purple a mixture of red and blue.

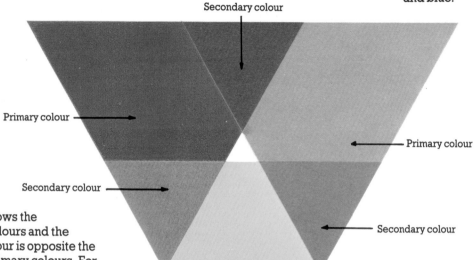

Secondary colour

Primary colour

Primary colour

Secondary colour

Secondary colour

Primary colour

Complementary colours

The colour triangle pictured on the right shows the relationships between the three primary colours and the three secondary colours. Each primary colour is opposite the secondary colour made by the other two primary colours. For example, red is opposite green on the triangle. These opposing pairs of colours are known as "complementary colours". Yellow and purple are complementary and so are blue and orange. Complementary colours look very vivid when used together.

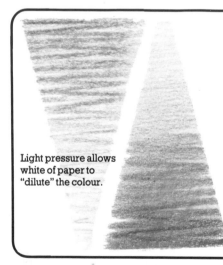

Light pressure allows white of paper to "dilute" the colour.

Colour tone

A colour's degree of lightness or darkness is called tone. Inks, paints and water-soluble crayons become lighter in tone when diluted with water. The tone of solid materials such as pencils and crayons will vary according to the pressure you use. By pressing hard you cover more of the paper and build up the colour. With light pressure you apply less colour and the white of the paper shows through, making it look lighter.

Heavy pressure builds up strong colours.

Colour illusion

If you stare at a coloured object for about thirty seconds and then look away to a white wall or piece of paper you will see a "ghost" image of the object. This image will not be the same colour as the original, but will be the colour which is complementary to it.

You can try this out by staring at the red cross. You should see a green ghost image.

Colours to choose

Although in theory you should be able to mix any colour, if you have just the three primary colours this is not possible in practice because the colours on sale are already mixtures. You need to buy a range of basic colours to work with. Aim to have at least two versions of each primary and secondary colour, such as the selection shown here. You will also

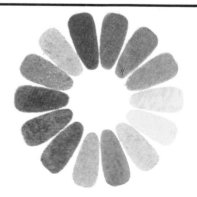

need some browns and greys and black and white. If you like to draw landscapes you will want lots of browns, ochres, greens and blues. For portraits, a range of yellows, flesh pinks and browns will be more useful. You can buy boxes of artists' pastels and paints which contain selections of colours chosen especially for landscapes or portraits.

Using colours together

You can create a feeling of warmth or coolness in a drawing by the careful use of colour. Blues, bluey greens and bluey mauves are cool colours which give a feeling of space and calm. Yellows, oranges and reds are warm colours which give a feeling of energy and life. Cool colours appear to recede and warm colours seem to come out of a drawing. Experiment to see if you can get different effects by drawing the same picture, first with warm colours and then with cool.

Colours affect each other when they are used together. A combination of similar colours gives a feeling of harmony but complementary colours contrast with each other.

If you use complementary colours together it is often better to use one as a main colour with small areas of its complementary, as in the picture below. Equal amounts of the two colours will fight for attention.

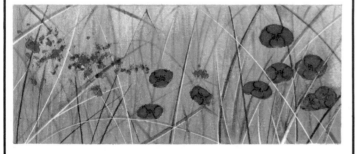

These coloured squares show how various colours can affect one shade of light blue, making it look different according to the colour it is surrounded by.

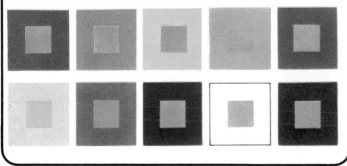

Water-colour washes

One way of getting colour into an otherwise black and white pencil or pen and ink drawing is by using washes of transparent inks or water-colour paint. You can either apply the wash to a finished drawing or paint it on to plain paper and then draw on top when it is dry.

Make a puddle of watery paint in a saucer or the lid of your paintbox, mixing it to the colour strength you want. Fix your paper to a drawing board and tilt it up at an angle so that the paint will run down the paper.

Ridge of paint.

Fill a large soft brush with paint and apply it across the paper in broad, even strokes in one direction. The paint will run slightly and form a ridge at the bottom of each stroke. Pick this up with the brush as you paint the next stroke.

Re-fill your brush whenever it runs out of paint. When you have covered the area you wanted to paint, wash and dry the brush and use it to mop up any paint at the bottom of the last stroke.

Use the same technique for applying small areas of wash.

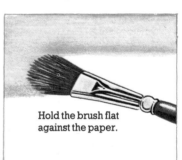

Hold the brush flat against the paper.

Stretching paper

Unfortunately a wash of watery paint makes some kinds of thin paper wrinkle and buckle as they dry. This should not happen if you apply only a small area of a light wash, or if you use thick paper such as water-colour paper. You can prevent ordinary thin paper from wrinkling by stretching it, before you apply a wash, in the way shown below.

Lay your paper flat on the drawing board or a smooth surface. Dip a sponge into some clean water, squeeze it out and use it to thoroughly wet the paper. Smooth the paper flat from the middle outwards to the edges without rubbing it.

Stick the wet paper to the board with strips of gummed brown paper tape, making sure that the paper is quite flat. Allow it to dry away from direct heat. The paper is now stretched and will not buckle if a wash is applied.

11

Coloured crayons

Coloured pencils and crayons can be used in much the same way as ordinary pencils. Start a picture with a very light, rough sketch either in lead pencil or a neutral coloured crayon such as grey. Build up your drawing as a whole rather than concentrating on just one part at a time. Try to avoid drawing outlines and filling them in with flat colour as this tends to look wooden and unrealistic. Shadows and highlights are just as important in a colour picture as in a black and white drawing.

These two pages explain how to use three different kinds of coloured crayons: coloured pencils, oil pastels and wax crayons.

Mixing new colours

It is impossible to mix two coloured crayons together to make a new colour before you use them, as they are solid. All colour mixing with crayons has to be done on the paper. You can control the colours that result by varying the kind of marks that you make and the pressure with which you use the crayon.

These pictures show some ways of colour mixing crayons on paper. The marks here are larger than you would normally use in a drawing, to make the technique shown more obvious.

Changing the pressure will alter the tone of the crayon. This is a good way of making a colour darker – mixing it with black often makes a dirty colour.

Rub the crayon gently on the paper even when you are trying to build up a dark tone. If you press too hard, you will indent the paper.

Shading two colours, one on top of the ▶ other, is a good way of making a smooth mixture of colours. By varying the pressure of one, or both, crayons you will alter the resulting colour.

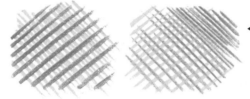

◀ Roughly cross-hatching one colour on top of an another is also very effective. Vary the distance between the sets of lines as well as the pressure for different effects and colours.

Try hatching several colours in the same ▶ direction. You can vary the length and number of lines in addition to the distance between them and pressure.

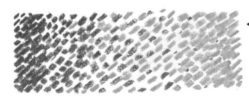

◀ You can mix colours by stippling little dots or dashes of them together, although it can take a long time to get the results you want. This method is often called "pointillism".

If you are using water-soluble crayons the ▶ colours will mix together if you put a wash of water over the lines.

How to use coloured pencils

Coloured pencils are probably the best choice for most colour drawing. They are convenient and easy to use and can produce several different effects. If you draw with well-sharpened pencils on smooth paper you will be able to get very fine, detailed results, like this drawing of flowers. By using rougher paper and pencils with a rounder or softer point you will get a looser, more grainy result.

When used extremely lightly, coloured pencil can be rubbed out with a putty eraser but a heavier mark will leave a stain on the paper. The softer kinds of pencil may smudge a little and sometimes finished drawings will need to be sprayed with fixative, but this depends upon the type of pencil and paper used.

This picture was drawn with ordinary coloured pencils on smooth paper.

Using oil pastels

Oil pastels are very soft and greasy. They make broad, opaque marks which can be built up into thick layers. You may find them rather difficult to handle at first especially if you are more used to pencil drawing techniques.

You may find it helpful to work standing up with your drawing board propped up almost vertical. Oil pastels are perfect for large drawings in a bold and vigorous style. Try using the whole of your arm as you draw, not just the hand and wrist, as this will help you to use the sweeping, bold strokes that suit oil pastels. Apply the crayons lightly at first as mistakes cannot be erased, although they are easy to cover up with more crayon later.

This picture was drawn with oil pastels on rough paper. The grain of the paper helps to give an impression of texture to the drawing.

Blending colours

Most oil pastels are made in strong, bright colours. They can be mixed in the ways shown on the previous page, or you can put one colour on top of another and blend them with the tip of a crayon or with your finger. The tips of the crayons get dirty as they pick up other colours from the picture, so wipe them with a clean rag after you have used them. You may find the colours too bright for the subtle effects of some landscapes and portraits.

Although oil pastels are soft and smudgy it is not usually necessary to spray the finished drawings with fixative. Fixative sometimes makes oil pastel marks dissolve and run.

Water-soluble crayons

Some coloured pencils and waxy textured crayons are water-soluble and can be used to give an effect similar to water-colour paints. If you put a very light wash of clean water over the lines it will soften and blur them or even wash them away to make a flat wash of colour. Try using this sort of crayon on dampened paper. The line will smudge and blur to make an interesting effect.

Blurred line of water-soluble crayon on dampened paper.

Using wax crayons

Wax crayons are paler in colour and harder than oil pastels. They do not make such thick, soft marks and can be sharpened to a point although it will not last very long. If used lightly and gently wax crayons make very grainy marks which allow the white of the paper to show through in a very effective way. You can take advantage of this by using wax crayons to make rubbings of textured objects.

Some colours are opaque and this will vary between different makes of crayon. Generally pale colours are transparent but dark coloured crayons are opaque and will cover others.

Charcoal, conté and pastels

These three materials are alike in several ways. They have a soft, chalky texture, are rather fragile and can be difficult to handle until you get used to them. It is probably a good idea to try out charcoal first if you are a beginner as it is cheap, quite easy to correct if you make a mistake and can create dramatic effects. All three materials are best suited to a bold, flowing style rather than precise detailed work.

You can use the same techniques for drawing with charcoal, conté and pastels and these are described below. Finished pictures should be fixed (see page 9) as they smudge very easily.

Making marks

This picture shows the different kinds of marks which can be made with conté, charcoal and pastel sticks. It is worth practising and trying out the techniques described here before you attempt a whole picture. The way in which you hold the stick and apply it to the paper determines the sort of mark that results. Vary the angle and pressure of the stick to get a different mark, but always begin with a very light stroke as too much pressure will clog the paper.

Setting up to draw

As these materials make a lot of dust and can be messy it is a good idea to wear old clothes. Work with your drawing board propped up at an angle, so that the dust falls away from your drawing. Try working with a short piece of conté, charcoal or pastel about 3 cm long, broken from the main stick. Long pieces tend to snap as you use them.

You can get very smooth tone and shading by gently smudging charcoal with your finger. Try this with pastel and conté too but do not overdo it as they are greasier than charcoal and tend to clog the surface of the paper and smear.

Keep your hand above the paper as you draw so that it will not smudge your drawing accidentally. If dust builds up, blow it away as brushing it with your hand will only smudge it into the paper.

If you are using pastels, leave them in their box or arrange them on a sheet of corrugated paper, in colour order, to stop them rolling around.

These materials are good for big pictures.

Pastels on a sheet of corrugated paper.

Use the sharp corners of square shaped sticks, like conté, to draw thin lines and dashes. With softer sticks, break off a small piece to get a sharp edge to use for thin lines.

Sharp-edged strokes made by a conté stick.

Broad, grainy conté mark.

Charcoal shading rubbed smooth with a finger.

Thin lines made with the edge of a conté stick.

Broad, heavy charcoal mark.

Broad strokes are made by using the stick on its side, varying the pressure to change the mark. Light pressure makes a grainy stroke. Conté is square-shaped and quite hard so it makes a sharper, harder-edged mark than charcoal.

Charcoal, conté and pastels are also made as pencils. These are less versatile than the sticks as they cannot make such a wide range of marks, but they are very useful for adding fine details to a picture. These pencils are often too large to fit into a sharpener so you should use a craft knife and then shape the point on sand-paper.

Choosing paper

These three materials show up the texture of the papers they are used on and so the paper you choose will alter the effect of your picture. Try out different rough and textured papers, such as rough water-colour and cartridge paper, sugar paper and pastel papers. Pastels must be used on paper with a rough surface, known as a tooth, as it holds the grains of pastel much better than smooth paper.

Papers are made in lots of colours and this is a way of introducing extra colour into a drawing. A mid-toned colour, such as pale grey or green, is a good choice as you can make marks on it which are lighter as well as darker. Very dark papers can be dramatic with white chalk or conté and pale pastels.

Highlights

Highlighting can be an interesting technique, especially with charcoal and conté. If you are drawing on white paper you can use the paper itself to make the highlights by leaving it uncovered. If you are using charcoal you can erase areas to reveal the paper with a putty eraser moulded to a point.

White conté, pastel or chalk are good for highlights on coloured papers. You can make highlights with bold strokes or by gently blending the white into the dark areas for a smooth graduated effect. Looking at black and white photographs will help you to see how shadows and highlights fall.

Black and white conté drawing on grey Ingres paper.

Making corrections

Charcoal is quite easy to remove if you make a mistake. Dust off as much of the powdery surface as possible with a soft cloth and then rub out the mark with a putty eraser.

Stiff paintbrush

Putty eraser

Conté and pastel are more difficult as they are slightly greasy and make a stain on the paper. Use a stiff paintbrush to lift off as much of the mark as you can, blowing away the resulting dust. Gently press a putty eraser against the mark to lift off more, taking care not to smudge the mark. Finally use the eraser to rub out the rest of the stain on the paper.

Drawing with pastels

This pastel picture of a seascape was drawn with soft pastels on rough water-colour paper. Begin a picture in the usual way with a rough sketch, using a neutral coloured pastel. Build up shapes and areas of colour rather than using outlines.

Always use pastels very lightly. They will break if you press too hard. The paper will only hold a certain amount of the pastel, so if you press heavily you will clog the paper and make it difficult to use another colour on top.

Mixing colours

Colour mixing is very important with pastels but you should be careful not to overdo it as too many colours on top of each other will make a muddy effect. Try the colour mixing techniques shown on page 12 and use small strokes and dashes of colour.

Good quality soft pastels are made in hundreds of colours as each main colour is produced in about eight grades from light to dark. It is best to start with a box of about 12 assorted pastels and add to them later when you can afford to.

Store pastels carefully as they are very fragile. Use the original box or, if you have loose pastels, keep them in a small box on a sheet of corrugated paper and protect them with a layer of cotton wool.

Drawing in pen and ink

If you want to make very crisp, clean and precise drawings, a drawing pen and ink are the best choice. You can use either dip or fountain drawing pens with changeable nibs of various widths. These nibs are flexible and so you can vary the flow of ink and the resulting line by changing your pressure on the pen.

Ink lines cannot be erased and so you should plan your drawings quite carefully before you start. Make a rough pencil sketch before you begin drawing in ink.

Here are some hints on using the different kinds of pens and inks which are available.

This drawing was done with a dip pen and India ink on smooth white cartridge paper. This is the best kind of paper to use for a sharp, clean effect.

Pens can only draw lines, dashes and dots, they cannot make soft tone and shading in the same way as pencils and crayons. The best techniques for making tone with a pen and ink are hatching, cross-hatching and stipple, although you can also use a wash of ink to make flat areas of solid shading.

Use your rough pencil sketch just as a guide for the pen lines. If you are not very confident about working in pen and ink, make a more detailed sketch and ink over it. Once you have got going you will find it much easier to work without pencil lines.

Pencil guide lines

Cross-hatching makes darker tone than just hatching.

Hatching lines

Draw hatching lines freehand. Using a ruler makes them look too severe and can cause smudging.

Dip pens

Dip pen

Dip pens are inexpensive and can be used with any kind of ink. They have to be dipped into the ink frequently and one drawback is that they may run dry in the middle of drawing a line. There is also a danger of making blots.

Fountain pens

Fountain pen

Rotring pen

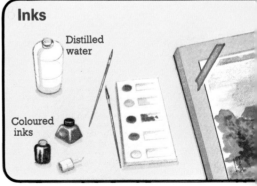

Inks

Distilled water

Coloured inks

Fountain pens are more convenient to use than dip pens but they cannot be filled with India ink or any other kind of waterproof ink as these contain a gum which will clog the pen. Always wash your pen with clean water when you finish

drawing or re-fill with a new colour.

Rotring type pens are often used for illustration and technical work as they draw a consistently even line. They should only be filled with special ink that is recommended by the manufacturers.

Inks are made in a range of brilliant, transparent colours. You can mix inks together before using them to make a new colour or use the techniques shown on page 12. Dilute ink with distilled water

As you cannot erase ink, you will have to draw over any mistakes. Do not worry about this too much, as wrong lines can often be less obvious once a picture is completely finished. If you want a very neat picture, plan it carefully before you start drawing.

Stippled dots make an area of light tone.

Wash of diluted Indian ink.

Washes of pale inks can look very effective on top of a pen and ink drawing and are a way of making areas of flat tone and shade. If you want to do this you must use waterproof ink for the original line drawing, otherwise the picture will run when you apply the wash. Make sure that the picture is completely dry before applying a wash.

Here, washes of diluted coloured inks have been brushed on top of waterproof Indian ink lines. You should build up the tone gradually with layers of wash.

You can use thick white poster paint on top of areas of dark ink for highlights.

Fibre tipped pens

Fibre tipped pens are made with a variety of tip shapes and sizes and in lots of bright colours. They draw flowing lines and are good for bold work. Some contain water-soluble ink and so can be used with a wash of water.

Ball point pens

Ball point pens glide over the paper with a smooth action and although they cannot make a huge variety of marks they can be useful. They contain a slightly smudgy ink made in a few bright colours.

Brush drawing

Water-colour brushes

Figure drawn with a brush and water-colour.

to make it lighter in colour.

Waterproof inks dry to a slightly glossy finish which will not run if wet ink or a wash is put on top. Non-waterproof ink will run if fresh ink or a wash is put on top.

You could try drawing with ink, or paint, using a brush instead of a pen. This produces a bold, flowing line and the effect can be varied by using different sized brushes, changing the consistency of the paint and by varying the pressure

on the brush.

Water-colour brushes with a pointed tip are probably the best to use. Always wash brushes thoroughly, especially if you have used waterproof ink, and re-form the point with your fingers.

Planning your pictures

One of the most important stages of drawing a picture is planning it before you start. Having decided what to draw, make some small, rough sketches on scrap paper to see which arrangement of objects or view of a scene you like the best. Arrange the largest objects first, without worrying about the small details.

Always be selective when composing a picture. You do not have to include every object or detail that you can see. Pictures can easily look over-full or cluttered. Leave things out if you think this will improve the composition. Experiment and try out your ideas with quick, rough sketches first.

Choosing what to draw

For some subjects composing a picture is just a matter of arranging the subject beforehand. With others you have to compose the picture by emphasizing some parts of a scene and omitting others.

You can compose a "still-life" picture by arranging the objects just as you want them before you start drawing. ▼

▲ Portraits are usually composed by the artist asking the model to sit or stand in a particular pose.

With outdoor scenes you have ▶ to walk around until you find a view you like and then decide which parts to concentrate on and which to leave out altogether.

◀ When drawing people unposed, you have less control over the composition than with a portrait. Concentrate on the general shape of a group, rather than on individuals.

You can use sketches and ▶ photographs to help you compose imaginative pictures. Experiment with different arrangements to see what effect each has.

Picture composition

Here are some drawings of the same subject, a football match, which show how you can get a different effect and feeling into a picture by altering the composition.

Bright colours help to focus interest in this part of the picture.

In this picture the match is a focus of interest although it is rather distant and almost a part of the general landscape. This composition is rather dull as the focus is in the centre and there is a lot of empty space around it.

Here the footballers are much closer and there is more feeling of involvement. It is often a good idea to make some of the figures overlap, otherwise they can look rather wooden and unnatural. Colour can also play an important part in a composition. The two players wearing bright red stand out against the grass and the other players.

Picture shape

Pictures can be any size and shape you want but this will also depend partly upon the subject you are drawing. Try out several different shapes and sizes by drawing quick, rough sketches. If your paper is not the right size and shape, draw a border on it in pencil and put your picture inside that.

Pencil border on paper to get required shape.

Landscapes and big scenes, like the picture above, usually fit best into a shape which is wider than it is tall. Portraits and full-length studies of people are best in a tall shape. Make sure that you can fit everything in when you do the rough, test sketch.

Using a viewfinder

Selecting part of a large outdoor scene can be very difficult. It is easy to try and put too much of a big view into your picture. You will find it easier to compose your picture if you use a cardboard viewfinder, like the one below, as it will isolate manageable parts of the scene. Look through the viewfinder with one eye closed.

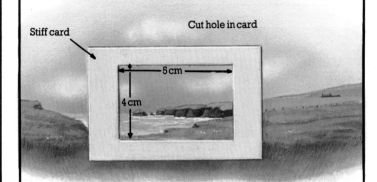

Stiff card

Cut hole in card

5 cm

4 cm

If you do not have a proper viewfinder with you, you can make a rough square with your thumb and forefinger and look through this to help you plan your drawing.

This is a more exciting composition as there is a feeling of action in the picture. The players are different sizes, which helps to give an impression of distance, and again bright colour is used to emphasize one player. The zig-zag, diagonal arrangement of the figures in the foreground helps to create a sense of movement and life.

A different paper shape needs a different composition. Here you are looking down at the scene so there is no sky or horizon. The diminishing size of the players leads the eye into the picture and gives it depth. Do not feel that you have to draw the whole of every figure.

Perspective

Perspective is a way of drawing which makes things look realistic and solid. It gives a picture an impression of depth and distance.

There are four basic rules of perspective and these are shown on the big picture below. You will probably be aware of them already, but it is important to remember to apply them when drawing a picture.

Colours change as they recede into the distance. They become less distinct and paler, taking on a bluish tinge. This is particularly important if you are drawing a landscape with a distant horizon, though less so if you are drawing a subject which is close to you.

Horizon   Vanishing point

Things look smaller the further away they are. These poles are, in fact all the same height, but the near ones look much larger than the far poles.

The amount of detail you can see decreases as the distance increases. These nearby trees look very distinct and detailed. The trees in the middle distance are still recognizable but are less detailed. In the far distance, close to the horizon, you can hardly distinguish any of the trees at all.

Parallel lines are the same distance apart all along their length and never meet. These railway tracks are parallel yet they look as if they get closer together and appear to meet on the horizon, because of perspective. The place where the lines seem to meet is called the "vanishing point". Vanishing points are always on the horizon.

1   View points

The horizon always appears to be at the artist's eye level. The horizon falls naturally about halfway up a scene looked at from a viewpoint at normal eye-level. Of course, you do not have to always draw the horizon in the centre of your pictures.

2

The horizon tends to fall higher if you look down from a high viewpoint. This picture shows a view from the top of a hill. There is little sky but a lot of ground and you can see a lot more of the scene than you would be able to from a normal standing height.

3

If you lie down on the ground the horizon will be very low. You will see a great deal of sky but very little ground. This viewpoint often gives you an unsatisfactory view of the scene as you will be looking up at most of the things around you.

Two point perspective

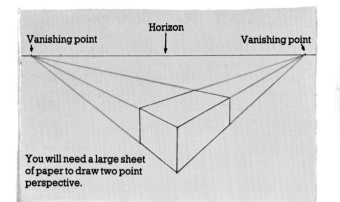

Vanishing point   Horizon   Vanishing point

You will need a large sheet of paper to draw two point perspective.

Lines above the horizon slope down to meet it.

Horizon

Lines below the horizon slope up to meet it.

The scenes on the previous page show the vanishing point of lines which are all parallel to each other. This is called "one point perspective". Most objects are made up of sides which point in different directions and so there will be two sets of parallel lines. Each set of lines will have its own vanishing point and this is called "two point perspective". The box above is shown with its two vanishing points.

Perspective is especially important when you are drawing buildings. Most buildings are a simple box shape, with a roof on top, which is quite easy to get right. Practise drawing simple boxes, viewed from various angles, with two point perspective. Continue the parallel lines until they reach the horizon. If you have got the perspective right, the lines will meet, making the vanishing points on the horizon.

It can be helpful to try and see objects with a more complex shape as though they were combinations of simple boxes. When you are making the rough, guide sketch for a picture, draw your subject like a box and round it out when you fill in the details later.

Circles in perspective

A circle in perspective looks oval and flattened. This shape is called an ellipse and it can be very difficult to draw correctly. Try to draw what you see, comparing the width of the ellipse with its height using the measuring technique

shown on page 7. You can also try drawing an ellipse inside a box (as for other complex shapes) but some people find this even more difficult than drawing the ellipse alone.

Circle

Ellipses

Compare height with width.

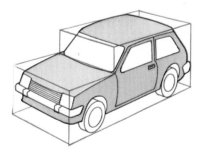

Using perspective

You can use perspective to help you work out how big things should be in the distance. This is useful if you are drawing from imagination where you cannot use the measuring technique as you can when drawing from life. The things you are drawing should all be of a similar size, for example people or cars as shown here.

To find the correct height draw one figure (or object) and the horizon. Lightly pencil in the figure's vanishing point anywhere on the horizon. Other figures of a similar height to the first will fit between the lines that join the top and bottom of the figure to the vanishing point.

You can use this technique to find out how wide something in the distance should be by drawing the lines horizontally along the ground to the vanishing point on the horizon.

Here, the horizon passes through all the figures at the same point – the waist. As the horizon is always at the artist's eye level the person who drew this must have been sitting down. If the artist had been standing the horizon would have crossed the figures at eye level.

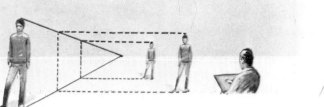

Drawing outdoors

Drawing out of doors has some practical difficulties. You have to find a scene that you want to draw and a comfortable place to work where you are not in anyone's way. You have to remember to take all the paper and equipment you will need with you. If it is windy you may have to tape down your paper to stop it blowing away. If it is sunny the reflection of the light on white paper may be dazzling and force you to sit in the shade.

Another problem is that the light changes as the day progresses and this alters all the shadows and colours. You may have to return to finish your picture another day.

Buildings

Towns are full of interesting buildings which are very good subjects to draw as they keep still and are a simple basic shape. Ordinary pencils are well suited to this subject as they can be used to draw fine details and also to represent textures such as stone and brick. Pen and ink will give a more precise and definite effect.

Use the measuring technique explained on page 7 and the rules of perspective on pages 20 and 21 to help you get your picture right.

Buildings often have interesting details such as doors, windows and decorations which make good pictures on their own.

Street scenes

Deciding what to draw and then choosing your view can be difficult. Large, dramatic and pretty scenes do not always make the best pictures. A street scene may be much more interesting and full of life. Do not feel that you have to put every part of a scene into a picture. Select the aspect you are most interested in and concentrate on that. A few well placed things look better than a jumble of bits and pieces.

In this ink drawing, the buildings are the most important part, although the people help to give the picture life.

Try to see glass and reflections as areas of tone and highlight and look for the general shapes they make.

People outside are usually walking and so are difficult to draw in any detail. Aim to get their proportions and the overall look right. Simple silhouettes can look effective.

Industrial scenes

Even an apparently ugly scene such as a building site or an industrial estate can be exciting to draw. Look out for the vast range of subtle colours in places which seem at first to be dull grey or black. You could find combinations of mauves, rust reds, greens and many other colours. You may also find interesting patterns and shapes formed by scaffolding or piles of bricks. This sort of scene can be drawn delicately, as shown here, with coloured pencils or more boldly with pastels or bright inks.

Look for patterns made by structures such as scaffolding or rubble.

Be careful of including things like vehicles as they might be moved away before you finish the picture.

Skies, clouds and water

Never leave the sky until last as it is an important part of any landscape. Work on it at the same time as the rest of the picture, looking at it as areas or shapes of tone and colour.

Concentrate on the general shape, size, tone and colour of clouds as they usually move too fast to draw in detail. Look at them as areas which contrast with the rest of the sky.

Try to see water as areas of tone or colour too. Look for the overall shapes made by waves, ripples and reflections. When you are drawing a reflection, remember that it will be a different shape from the real object as it is reflected from a viewpoint different from yours. The size and colours of reflections are usually different from those of the real object too, so draw reflections carefully to get them right.

Landscapes

Large views, especially in parks or the countryside, can often be difficult to compose. Use a viewfinder to help you and try to find a focus of interest for a picture. It is a good idea to include something like a path or river which will lead the eye into the drawing.

The lighting is a vital part of any scene and will affect the mood and feeling of a picture. Here, the dark sky and thundery light give this pencil drawing of an ordinary park a mysterious, intense air.

This path helps to lead the eye into the picture.

Parks are good places to draw as they are full of interesting details such as flowers, trees, ponds, sculpture and animals.

Detailed studies

A close-up, detailed study of an object, such as this gate latch, often makes a good picture. Look out for interesting textures in fallen trees or driftwood and the interesting shapes of unusual stones and other natural objects.

Drawing trees

When drawing trees, look for the overall shape of the particular tree and for the spaces between the branches which let light through. It is better to get the massed shape of the leaves right than to try and get a leaf "effect" with dashes and dots.

Distant leafy trees and bushes make a solid shape of tone or colours.

Bare, winter trees are a network of interwoven branches and twigs with lots of spaces in between. Concentrate on the main branches and general shape. Trying to draw every twig will just look messy.

Landscape patterns

Look out for the main patterns and shapes in a landscape. Ploughed fields, clumps of trees, grass and so on often look like areas of texture and you can draw a landscape in a way which emphasizes this feature, as in the pen and ink picture above.

Still life

When drawing a still life you have complete control over the choice and arrangement of your subject and lots of time to draw it. This is good practice to help you learn how to observe and draw things carefully and it gives you the chance to try out new drawing materials and to experiment with new techniques.

Setting up a still life

The arrangement of the objects for a still life is very important. Do not use too many things–five is usually enough. Put them together in a balanced way, not too far apart and not too squashed together.

Make sure that some of the objects overlap, otherwise the arrangement will look too posed. Keep changing the composition until you find one that you like.

Choosing your subject

Almost anything makes a good subject for a still life drawing. You may find an interesting arrangement of objects or an unusual subject by accident, such as a pile of clothes, a bowl of fruit, a collection of books or even a pair of old boots.

If you want to arrange a still life, it is often a good idea to start with a theme, food for example, and then choose objects which relate to it. An arrangement of carpentry tools or parts from an old clock could make a good composition.

It is best to keep the background quite empty and uncluttered at first. Try using a sheet of paper or some cloth as a backdrop to isolate the still life from its surroundings.

This still life on the theme of food was drawn on rough water-colour paper with soft coloured pencils.

These objects were arranged on a table which is the usual height for a still life. You could try changing your viewpoint by arranging your objects on the floor so that you look down at them, or on a high shelf so that you look up.

Lighting effects

You can arrange your own lighting using a reading lamp or desk light positioned about a metre away from the objects. Experiment by moving the lamp around to see what effects you get.

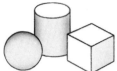

Lighting from the front can look harsh and make the objects appear flat, as there are few shadows.

Back lighting is not very satisfactory as the front of the objects will be in deep shadow.

Side lighting from slightly above or below gives the best effect. The shadows and highlights help to define the shape and form of the objects.

Negative space

Start a still life by roughly sketching the objects in position, using the measuring technique (page 7) to get the proportions right. It can help to look at the objects as if they were simple, flat shapes at this stage. Pay attention to the shapes of the spaces in between the objects too. This is called the "negative space" and it is as important to your drawing as the actual objects.

Practise drawing the spaces between objects by using areas of flat colour. You can build up the outline of an object by drawing the space around it.

One colour still life

An interesting project to try with charcoal, ordinary lead pencils or black ink, is to set up a still life composed only of white objects. Choose things with different textures to introduce some variation. Where two objects meet, or overlap, there will be a contrast between their tones, although they are the same colour.

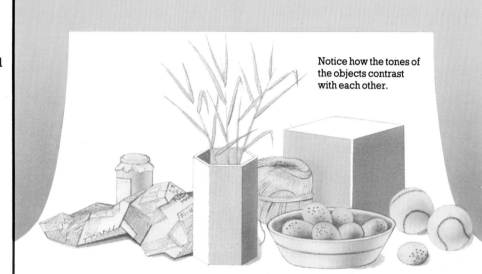

Notice how the tones of the objects contrast with each other.

You can try a similar experiment using colour by setting up a still life using, for example, only red or green things.

Do not use outline but rely on subtle graduated colours and tones to build up the picture.

Drawing natural objects

Natural objects such as shells, stones, driftwood, plants and vegetables make very good subjects for still life studies. They usually have interesting shapes, textures and colours which are more challenging to draw than those of manufactured objects.

Ordinary or coloured pencils are a good choice for this sort of drawing as they can be used in a very light and sensitive way to capture the details of the objects.

Vegetables often make good patterns when sliced in half.

Drawing larger than life

In most drawings you are making things, such as people or buildings, look far smaller than they really are. It can be exciting to draw small objects like beans, sweets, keys, pins and so on, very much bigger than life size. You will need to study your subject closely and carefully to do this.

Drawing people

Drawing people is just like drawing other things. You need to look hard at your subject and draw what you see rather than your idea of what a figure or face looks like. Poor drawing is obvious when you are drawing people, as your picture will not look like your model. It is best not to worry about getting a likeness at first, as this will gradually come as the drawing progresses. If you can get the size, position and proportions of the features right, your drawing will probably be a fair likeness. Try not to concentrate on drawing one feature or part of the body in detail, but work on the figure as a whole.

The materials you use will affect the style of your drawing. Pencil is a good choice if you want a detailed drawing and have a lot of time. Charcoal is effective for bold pictures and quick sketches of people in action.

Although you can work from photographs, it is best to have a live model to draw. You could ask a friend or relative to pose for you. Choose a comfortable position and do not expect a model to sit for more than 15 minutes without a rest. You can also try drawing people unposed, say when they are sitting reading, watching television or sewing but they may move before you have finished.

Keep the background uncluttered and simple so that it is not distracting.

Notice how the parts of the body fit together. The head rests at an angle on the cylinder of the neck, which is itself joined to the shoulders at an angle.

Work with your drawing board propped up so that you can stand back and compare your drawing to the model.

The human figure is a complicated arrangement of many shapes and it can help to try and see it in a simplified form. Imagine the head as an egg shape and the limbs and torso as cylinders with swivelling joints, as in the figure above. Use this simplified form when drawing rough guide sketches.

Measuring and comparing

The measuring method described on page 7 will help you to get the proportions of a figure correct.

Although people vary a great deal in size and shape, you will find that an adult's total height is about seven times the height of the head and neck. It is a good idea to lightly pencil the head and body proportions of your model on the paper and then draw within this framework. The total height of a seated figure is about five times the height of head and neck.

Children's heads are bigger in proportion to their bodies than adults'. This varies with age.

Compare each part of the body to other parts and to the figure as a whole. Compare the lengths and the thickness of limbs and look to see how parts of the body line up with each other both horizontally and vertically.

Always look and measure carefully as different poses change the relative sizes and positions of the parts of the body. Also look for the shapes of any spaces between the torso and the limbs.

People in perspective

When drawing people, you do not have to draw the whole of the figure with the same amount of detail. You may want to concentrate more on the head and face than the legs and feet, as in the pencil drawing below.

Perspective applies as much to people as to other objects. Parts of the body which project towards you will be "foreshortened". This means that they will appear shorter than they really are.

Try emphasizing the foreshortening of parts which project by drawing them with darker and thicker lines.

Clothes

Clothes help to give a figure solidity and shape and can be very interesting to draw in themselves. Look to see how different kinds of materials hang, fold or crease to form shadows and highlights. Try using shading techniques such as stipple and hatching to show the texture of the cloth. It is better to do this in small areas as it would look messy if applied all over.

Stripes of sweater help to show the rounded shape of the figure.

Small areas of shading gives the impression of the sweater's texture.

Shading

Shadows and highlights are extremely important as they help to make a figure look solid and realistic. Look to see how shadows follow the shapes of the body, gradually changing in tone.

Movement

It is particularly difficult to draw people when they are moving. You can try using photographs or ask your model to keep repeating a simple movement, such as a hop or step. This will help you to train your eyes to catch the particular action you want to draw. A rough bold sketch can sometimes have a better feeling of action than a detailed drawing.

Shoulders and hips are rarely in a straight line but are usually sloping.

Angular, zig-zag shapes help to give a feeling of action and movement.

Balance

Whatever position a person is in, their body is always balanced. If they move one limb, they also move the rest of their body slightly to re-balance their weight. When you are drawing a figure, try to imagine how it would feel to be in that pose. This can help you to get the balance right in your picture.

Portraits

Portrait drawing can seem rather daunting, especially when you are a beginner. If you do not want to test your skill on a friend try a self-portrait. This will give you lots of time to work on the picture and you will be able to concentrate without worrying about your model. Set up a mirror so that you can see yourself without having to move your head.

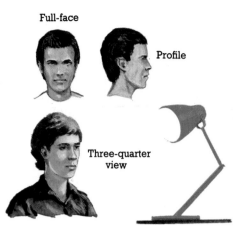

Full-face

Profile

Three-quarter view

1 Start a portrait with a rough, egg-shaped sketch of the whole head without any features or hair. Use the measuring technique (see page 7) to work out where on the head the features should be positioned.

2 You may be surprised to find that the eyes are positioned half-way down the head. Beginners often put the eyes much too high up, on the forehead.

Pencil in two very light guide lines, one down through the nose and the other across the face through the eyes. These lines should curve to follow the round shape of the head and will help you to put the features in the right places.

Look at how the features line up with each other. The ears often line up with the eyes and mouth, for example. Draw rough guide lines to plot these relationships.

Drawing hair

It is best to treat hair as an overall shape enclosing the head. Do not try to draw every strand and curl but put in a few if they look interesting. Look out for areas of light and dark and notice how the hair hangs and follows the shape of the head in different places. You could try out various methods of shading to draw hair.

Nose and mouth

Try to see the nose and mouth as areas of light and shade rather than drawing them in outline. The darkest part of the mouth is the line between the two lips and it can help to draw this first. The top lip is often in shade and so is darker than the bottom lip which may look pale if it is catching the light.

The tip and nostrils are often the most clearly defined parts of the nose. Try to draw the length using only tone and highlights to show its shape and size.

Choosing a pose

When you are drawing a self-portrait it is difficult to do anything other than a full-face view. With a model you can choose a more interesting pose. A three-quarter view is often the best, a profile can look rather severe.

Lighting is an important part of a portrait. Use a desk lamp so that you can move it around and experiment with the strength and direction of the light. Make sure that your model is comfortable and not dazzled by the light.

3 It is the positioning and relative proportions of the features which give a face its character, so if you can get these right your picture should look like your model. Keep comparing the size and positions of the features with each other and lightly sketch them in with the help of the guide lines.

4 Once you have all the features in the right places you can start to draw in more detail. Do not try to draw one part, say an eye, in detail before you have roughly sketched in the rest. Build up a portrait gradually, like any other drawing, looking for areas of light and shade on the face.

Eyes

The eye is a round ball, sunk in a hole in the skull, so there is often an area of shadow around the eyes. The lids cover most of the eyeball and follow its rounded shape. The top of the pupil is covered by the upper lid.

The bottom of the pupil often rests on, or is just above the lower lid. Eyes always reflect light and it is important to draw these shiny highlights as they help to give life and expression to a portrait.

Upper lid

Pupil

Lower lid

The eyes are usually roughly one eye's width apart. Show the eyelashes as a soft, dark line, rather than trying to draw individual lashes.

Skin tones

It can be difficult to get convincing skin colours with coloured crayons. Try using just one or two colours and concentrate on the tones at first.

Drawing animals

Animals move about quickly and cannot be posed, which makes them difficult subjects to draw. If you want to do a detailed drawing, you will probably need to use photographs but sketching from life is very useful as it helps you to become familiar with an animal's structure and characteristics.

Aim to capture the overall shape and proportions of each animal. Look to see how it stands and moves. Some animals have limbs which bend backwards when compared with human limbs. Different kinds of animals have different characteristics. Cats, for example, are lithe and slinky while horses are more angular and stiff.

Getting these impressions right, as well as the more obvious details will make a picture more convincing.

Drawing pets

Pets are a good choice to start with as you will already be familiar with their shape, patterns and characteristics. Try drawing them when they are asleep or eating, as they will be still for a while then. Start by drawing the head, body and limbs as simple egg or cylinder shapes to get the positions and proportions right. Lightly sketch in more details, building up areas of tone and highlight to make the pattern of the markings and show the texture of the fur or skin.

Begin with a light rough, guide sketch.

Soft pencil, conté and charcoal are good for sketching animals. You can create the effect of glossy fur or textured skin, with practice.

The pattern of markings will follow the shape and line of the body.

Look to see how animals hold their heads and limbs.

Drawing birds

Birds form two quite different kinds of shape. They are compact egg-shapes when perched but make a series of wide, streamlined shapes as they flap their wings when flying. This makes a flying bird hard to draw, but look for the general shape of the wings and tail. A bird identification book will help you to know what to look for. It is probably best to do quick sketches.

Perching birds are two small egg-shapes with the wings and tail sticking out.

This bird has big wings and distinct dark markings.

The tail is striped and triangular.

Wing feathers make a jagged shape.

Animal proportions

If an animal is standing still, you will be able to draw it with the help of the measuring technique (page 7). Compare the various parts of the body to each other and put rough guide lines on your sketch to help you.

Animals usually have two heights, the height from ground to shoulder and the height from ground to head.

Look to see which parts of the body line up vertically and horizontally.

Compare the length of the whole body with the head, the legs and the height.

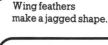

Where to draw animals

Zoos and museums are good places to visit if you want to draw unusual animals. Quick sketches are best in zoos if the animals are active, but the stuffed animals displayed in museums will give you the chance to do more detailed drawings.

29

Drawing from imagination

Drawing pictures from imagination can be great fun, but you may find it rather disappointing if you cannot put down on paper what you "see" in your head. Try to train your memory so that you can recall the colours, shapes and proportions of things that you see. It is also useful to use photographs and sketches for reference if you want your pictures to be realistic in style.

If you do not want to draw in a realistic style you could experiment with abstract ideas and different drawing styles. Ink blots, doodles and rubbings made with a crayon could all be the starting point for an abstract or realistic imaginative picture.

Realistic scenes

This imaginative space moonscape looks realistic because it follows the rules of perspective which apply to real scenes. It is very important to decide where the light in a picture is coming from so that you can make the shadows and highlights look correct.

Strange colours

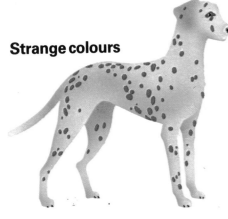

Drawing things in a realistic style but with dramatically altered colours or patterns can produce an interesting picture. You can also try changing the texture of your subject.

Perspective tricks

Deliberately ignoring the rules of perspective when drawing a scene will create a weird and amusing picture, like this one. The style is realistic but the result is not.

Distorted sizes

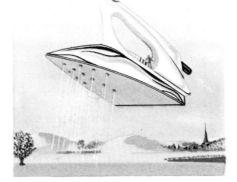

Changing the relative sizes of some realistically drawn objects can make a dramatic picture. An unusual combination of ordinary objects can also produce a strange but fascinating picture.

Unusual techniques

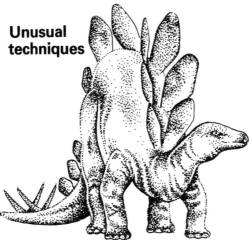

You could try drawing a picture using only one kind of line. This monster was drawn using only dots but you could try using only straight or wiggly lines.

Patterns

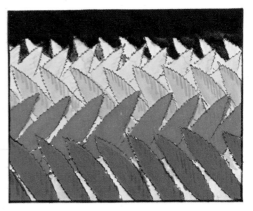

The patterns, shapes and colours of real objects may give you ideas for abstract or imaginative pictures. This repeating design was developed from rubbings of autumn leaves.

Mounting drawings

Once you have drawn some pictures you are pleased with, you may want to hang them up on display. Drawings can be framed like paintings but often look best in a simple card mount like the one described here. Card mounts are quite easy and cheap to make. You will need some thick card as a backing, thinner card for the window frame, a metal ruler, a set-square, masking tape and a craft knife with changeable blades. If you decide to frame a drawing you can buy special kits from art stores.

Masking tape for fixing mount together. (Glue or ordinary sticky tape will damage the card and drawing.)

Thin, coloured card for the window frame of mount.

Set-square

Thick, strong card to use for backing of the mount.

Craft knife with spare sharp blades.

Use string to hang the picture.

Metal ruler for cutting straight edges in card.

1

Look at your drawing and decide which area of it you want to be seen through the window frame of the mount. Mark this lightly on the drawing in pencil. Then decide on the overall size and shape of the finished mounted drawing.

2

Backing card

Cut the backing card to the dimensions you have decided on for the finished mount, checking that the corners are square with the set-square.

Put the drawing on the backing and move it around until it looks right.

3

Masking tape

Pictures usually look best if the top border is narrower than the bottom one. Check that the two side borders are equal in size and then fix the drawing to the backing card with a strip of masking tape in each corner.

4

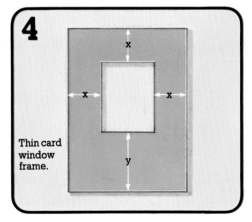

Thin card window frame.

Cut the window frame card to the overall finished size. Lightly pencil in borders to match the measurements round the drawing on the backing card. Cut out the middle to make the window, using the craft knife and ruler.

5

Masking tape hinge.

Attach the top edge of the window frame to the top edge of the backing card using a strip of masking tape to make a hinge, as shown above. Fold the frame down to cover the backing card and the mount is finished.

Cutting tips

Very thick card is difficult to cut neatly so use thin card for the window frame.

Use a new, sharp blade in your knife and rest on a hard, smooth surface when cutting card to make sure you get a clean edge.

When cutting the middle out of the window frame, rest the ruler over the border, as in the picture below, so that if the knife slips it will only cut the waste card in the middle.

Always take great care when using your craft knife.

Going further

Looking at other artists' work can be very helpful and once you have become familiar with the various drawing techniques and materials you will be able to see which an artist has used in a picture. You can see collections of drawings, and paintings, in art galleries, museums and art centres, or try looking at reproductions of pictures in art books. The *World of Art* series (Thames and Hudson) and the *Dover Art Library* series (Dover) have books about individual artists and sometimes show drawings as well as paintings. *Drawing Ideas from the Great Masters* by Frederick Malins looks at the drawings of many famous artists.

You will probably also find it useful to read more books aimed at helping you learn to draw. Some books cover all aspects of drawing, others concentrate on one kind of material such as pastels, or on one kind of subject, such as drawing animals. Look for books in your local library and art supply store as well as in book stores.

Here are some books which may help you develop your drawing beyond the basic stages explained in this book.

Drawing by Janet Allen (Marshall Cavendish).
The Complete Drawing Book edited by Peter Probyn (Studio Vista).

The Pitman *Draw* series has a general book called *Draw in Pencil, Charcoal, Crayon and Other Media* by Hans Schwartz. Other books in this series concentrate on particular subjects.
How to Draw and Paint edited by Stan Smith (Ebury Press) is expensive but well worth looking at for its very comprehensive step-by-step approach.
Portrait Drawing Techniques by Dianne Flynn and *Landscape Drawing* by John O'Conner (Batsford).
Using Pastels by Joan Scott (Warne's Observer's Guides).
Learn to Paint with Pastels by John Blockley (Collins).
Pastels for Beginners by Ernest Savage (Studio Vista).

Index